I0536625

Trained Thoughts Publishing Presents

You are single

until you're married

Almondo Scott

Table of contents

Part 1: Introduction

Spontaneous is fun and sexy

Believe nothing you hear, but everything you see and half of what someone tells you.

First, keeping a marriage spicy is the best way to keep it together and strong. Being spontaneous is fun and sexy plus it helps you to figure out your mate to the point that you know what they like, what turns them on, and how they like to be treated. plus, it will help you to physically feel them out, but no matter how long you are in a relationship, technically you are single until you're married.

Part 2

Trusting your mate is key

So, Choice tells Samantha that he is going to go play basketball with the fellas and he will be back shortly. She says, "Cool, I want to run to the store anyway, so I will see you when you get back." Then she asks him if she could borrow his car because her car needs brakes and when she stops, she hears squeaking, he says "Okay, no problem." Samantha is new to the neighborhood, so she has not figured out certain routes to get from point a to point b, so she gets lost a lot. She decide to use the gps to find her way to the store because she got tired of driving in circles. She puts the store in the GPS, and that is when she noticed a location that was already saved in his locator, and it was a home addressee. She looked confused but curious, so instead of going to the store, she opened the GPS locator to the location that was already saved and decided to drive to see where it would lead her and a home addressee it was. She parked a couple of houses back and just sat there to see what she would get out of being nosy. In addition to her surprise, she sees her man coming out of one of the houses. Surprised, mad, pissed, angry, furious, outraged and basically hurt. Every word that could describe a woman's feeling after seeing her man in one place when he said he would be somewhere else, that just raised a red flag... because he lied.

She waits to see him get in a car then she makes a U-turn and rushes to the house to beat him there. When he walks into the house, she confronted him saying, "How was your workout?" She asked. He replied, "It was a great workout." She then asked, "Was the pussy as good as the workout or was that the workout?" He looked at her in shock and responded, "What are you talking about?" She said nothing. #niggasdodumbshit

Days passed, and Samantha never brought back up what happened again. Meanwhile, they were in the house one-day trying to figure out what they were having for dinner and choice asked Samantha if he could see her phone because his phone had died, and he wanted to call to order some food to be delivered since no one wanted to cook.

While Choice was in google looking for a restaurant, a message popped up that read Adam from the job.

"Can I see you tonight?" Choice was shocked but decides to reply.

"Yes, where are we meeting up at and what time."

"Asap, the motel next to the job."

After he messaged Adam back, Samantha walks into the room.

"We need to talk," Samantha says.

"You got damn right, we do, your ass ain't shit." Choice says while holding her phone.

She snatches her phone from him and looks at it, then looks at him.

"Wait, did you just reply to a message someone sent me? Wow," as she laughs. "That's what we on huh."

"Seems like it to me."

"Okay so, how long you been fucking her?" Samantha asks as she folds her arms.

"Just as long as you and Adam from the job been meeting at the motel by the job."

"Wow." Samantha says as she smiles and giggles.

So, Samantha sits down and ask Choice a question.

"So, how long have you been fucking her and how many times have you been over her house?"

Choice looks at her and smiles.

"How many times have ya'll met up at the motel by your job and had sex?"

"Omfg, why you are asking a question with motherfukker question, dude just answer what I asked you, shit." Samantha says in frustration.

"The same reason you are not answering the question I asked you?" Choice asks.

"Lmao, okay I'm going to be very honest with you, yes, I have met him at the motel a couple of times, but we never did anything until you started accusing me of cheating. So, the last two times we did had sex. But it was only because you were accusing me of doing something that I was not doing, so I said since I'm being accused of cheating and I am not, why not do it I'm already being accused of it anyway."

Choice face freezes as he stands there with his hand on his chin in shock as Samantha sits there with the shit face before she asks him. "Okay, so what about that chick house I saw you coming out of the other day?"

Then he sits down next to her and smiles.

"Yes, I have been to her house several times and yes, we had sex the first time I went over there but after that, we did nothing we just chilled."

"Do you like her?"

"I wouldn't say I like her, but I care for her."

"Do you have feelings for him?"

"Over time I have grown feelings for him because he listens and pays attention to me." Samantha says.

"Wait, how did you find out where she lives? For the record, I only dropped her off 2 times."

Choice says while laughing and looking at Samantha as she smiles.

"So, was that her in the car with you the other day on the expressway."

That comment left the most shocking look on Choice face, but he still smiles.

"Yes, it was but, how in the hell you know that?"

"Don't worry about it asshole, just know I saw your fake slick ass."

Samantha says with aggression as she slaps him in the back of the head and walks into the kitchen.

Choice looks at her and laughs as he gets up and goes into the kitchen with her.

"Okay, so when you said you were at the bar with the girls, was that him you were dancing with up on all night?" Choice asks.

"Yea, but wait a fucking minute how in the hell you know that?" Samantha asks while laughing.

"Don't worry about it you piece of shit, just know I was there." Choice says as he walks away.

They look at each other laughing. She walks in the washroom and he walks into the bedroom, they put their clothes on, and he leaves the house laughing the whole time while walking out the house, as Samantha is in the bedroom getting ready before she leaves out. After three days pass by, while they are sleeping, Choice phone vibrates at 5:45 am, she rolls over and looks at him, he moves like he is about to wake up, but he continues sleeping so she looks to see who is messaging him so damn early in the morning, she sees it's a female. She decides not to open the message, she just showers, gets her dress on, and heads out to work, to her surprise Choice is already out when she gets out of the shower.

You see, today is Samantha's birthday, so she says to herself, 'today is my birthday I have no time for the bullshit'. She gets out the bed and goes to shower, as Choice walks in and gets in the shower with her and kisses her as they had birthday sex. Then he goes out after he finishes washing up, while she stays in. She goes to the room, to see a birthday card on the dresser, with a dozen roses and a pandora bag. She smiles as she opens the closet to get her clothes and about twenty balloons flew out. She smiles again before she finishes getting her dress on as she gets in her car and drives to work. As soon as she gets to work there was another dozen of roses with a card sitting on her desk that says happy birthday beautiful enjoy your day but didn't say who it was from, so without even thinking she calls Choice.

"Thank you again baby I appreciate it, and you really outdid yourself this time." Samantha says.

"Aw, your welcome baby anytime." Choice says.

"This has been a great morning so far, from the house to what I received at work, just curious how you pulled it off but I'm grateful."

"House okay but work, what are you talking about."

Samantha pause and keeps quiet as he continues saying hello as she didn't answer him but she hangs up as she sits there trying to figure out what she just did while beating herself up for assuming it is him without knowing if he actually did it.

So, Choice calls Samantha back:

"I think I lost connection and why were you so overly excited when you said thank again?" Choice asks.

"Because you are so good to me and I really love you." Samantha says while on the other side of the phone she is making a what the fuck did I just do face.

"Aw okay love you too." Choice says as he gets in his car and heads up to Samantha's job to surprise her and take her to lunch. Soon as he walks into her job, he sees her, and a guy was already having lunch in the breakroom. So, he leaves out and heads back to the car. Then he received a message from Alicia.

"He at work now so come get this pussy."

The look on his face is priceless, he sits there and thinks about that text on Samantha's phone earlier, so he started his car back up and goes to Alicia house to get that pussy.

So, after Samantha and Adam finish lunch, he gives her some birthday head and a quickie in the storage closet. Meanwhile, when Choice begins leaving Alicia house that's when he notices a work badge, the same one that Samantha has but the name said Adam on it as he looks up and puts his hand on his head. Come to find out Alicia is married, and he has no idea because she stands by the don't ask don't tell policy. All he knows is her name; Alicia Staples and he hears Samantha on the phone one day saying, "Okay Mr. Staples, I will come in early." He laughs, smiles, and laughs again. Adam doesn't wear his ring at work, so when his pants fall while they are fucking, his ring and his ID fall out as they are getting it hard in the storage closet. She sees his ring and said to herself, 'wtf he married', she decides not to say anything to him but once he leaves, she just put the ring and ID in her pocket. She thought to herself 'I can't get mad because they have the don't ask don't tell policy still applies as well'.

Part 3

Men ain't shit, but women worst

So, Adam wedding ring falls out of his pocket while they are in the storage closet, Samantha finds it after he is out and now Samantha feels like he has some explaining to do. Meanwhile, Alicia and Adam are having a lunch date and their conversation begins to get interesting.

"Have I ever done something so bad that you wanted to cheat on me?" Adam asks.

"Yea, but if I'm going to cheat it's going to be because I want to not because of nothing you did."

"Well damn." Adam says while grinning.

"I'm just being honest." Alicia replies as she shrugs her shoulders.

"Yea, I did ask for that." Adam says.

"Okay have you ever cheated on me?" Alicia asks Adam as he starts smiling.

"Yes and no." Adam says after laughing.

"I figured that because you are just like most men stupid enough to cheat, but dumb enough to get caught." Alicia says while laughing.

"You funny as hell."

Then Alicia's phone rings, she looks at it and grins then look at Adam with a shocking face, then Adam gets a message looks at it then sips his tea and looks up and see Alicia is looking at him.

"Are you going to reply to that message?" Alicia asked him.

"Yea, as soon as you answer that call." Adam replies.

They both ignore the text and the call and continues conversing with each other before ordering their food. After eating, they talk for a little while before leaving the table to go to the washroom. And soon as Adam goes into the washroom, Choice calls Alicia and she answers.

"Hello."

"What's happening Ms. Staples?"

"Oh, wow, hey Mr. relationship."

"Why you didn't tell me you were married."

"You're funny but the same reason you didn't tell me you were in a relationship; you didn't ask I didn't tell."

Choice laughs.

"And plus, when I came up to my husband's job and saw him all hugged up all on your girl, I am like oh hell yea, so I kept my cool and kept quiet and did what I did."

"Wait a minute, so what you are telling me right now is, you plotted on me." Choice says in shock.

"Um duh, I'm like I seen her guy before at the gym of 12th street a couple of times before."

"Your sneaky ass really did plot on me, wow."

"Naw I'm just slicker than most men are, plus I was just doing me, that's all."

"Hey, give me one second, I need to take care of something I'm going to hit you back."

"You good take your time."

Samantha messages Adam and tells him they need to talk, and he replies ok, then she calls

"What's up, Miss Lady?"

"Hey, did you lose something?"

"He laughs oh damn my work ID, why you found it or something."

"Is that before or after I say the other half of what I want to ask you."

"Lmao, yea my wedding ring too, but I am not too sure where that's at right now."

"I have both of them, but why wasn't I told that you were married and why did I have to find out this way."

"You never asked me, so I was thinking it wasn't a concern to you."

"Oh, it's no concern, but didn't think you were married, and if you were you could have told me."

"Well, good thing you are not being paid for thinking, and why do you care now."

"I don't, and don't get smart motherfukker." Samantha says with aggression.

"I'm not I am just curious how you got it without me noticing it was gone."

"You slipping playa, but you dropped them both in the storage closet, I guess when your pants hit the floor from being a damn freak."

"Thanks, appreciate but give me a second let me hit you have to get back to the wife."

"Okay, cool."

Adam comes out of the washroom and runs into Alicia as she comes out of the women's room as they head to the exit and stare at each other every 5 minutes while driving in silence all the way home.

So, once they make it to the house they get out of their clothes and decide to watch a movie before going to sleep because they both have to go to work the next day.

Now it's Wednesday morning, and that means, Samantha's long day at work, so to be a good man Choice decides to pick her up from work so they can go on a date

In addition, he tells her to leave her car at the job. So, he decides to drive to take a load off her when they go to the movies. However, she isn't tired from work, only tired from putting in work.

Part 4

Explain Yourself

Before leaving out for work, Alicia sits back and reflects on everything that has taken place in the last couple of days, she wants to do something nice for her man. So, she decides to surprise him at his job and take him to dinner after he gets off work because he has mentioned several times how he wants to try Pappadeaux. Only if she knows that by the time she gets to him he probably would have eaten already. So, she texts him if he wants to go to Pappadeaux.

Alicia wants to finish the conversation going on between her and Adam on the other date, but a misunderstanding brings about to complete silence on the way home.

Meanwhile, Choice looks at Showtime's for the movie and also makes plans for after the movie. Then calls Samantha and ask her if she wants to go to the movies.

"Sure, what time?" Samantha inquired.

"Why does that matter punk?" Choice replies.

"Really, come on now you know this my late night, stop being an idiot."

"Okay, around 9."

"Okay, that's cool, I can make that happen."

"Fosho see you in a little while."

"Okay baby."

Meanwhile, Alicia text Adam and asks him if he would rather call in the order to takeout and go back home to finish talking but before she could send the message, he texts her and tells her he has to work late because his relief called off.

So, Alicia and Choice both are trying to surprise their mates at their job. They pull up in the parking lot at the same time, they are far away, but right across from each other, so they could literally see each other vehicles so Alicia decides to see if this is really him, so she calls him.

"What's up dude?" Alicia says.

"What's happening?" Choice replies in shock.

"Nothing, what are you doing?"

"About to pick up the misses, wyd."

"At hubby job waiting on him to get off work."

"Wait, is that your car parked up there next to that red van?"

"Yea, is this you sitting over there in front of me with your interior lights on."

He turns the light off

"Yea, wait hold the fuck up."

"Are you fucking serious?"

Alicia hangs up the phone and Choice drops his phone on the passenger seat.

The two of them come out of their cars and begin walking towards each other and meeting up in the middle of the parking lot.

"Wait, are you telling me you up here to meet up with the misses?"

Choice smiles and giggles.

"But wait you said you were meeting up with hubby."

"Yea, my husband works here, why you seem surprised."

"Because I am, and this is a coincidence that we both here, at the same time for the same reason."

As they look at each other and then hearing sounds of laughter, they both look in the direction of the exit sign. After hearing a door close, they see a man walking backward saying come on sweetie with your silly ass, then Alicia sits on her car, as Choice stands next to her as the double doors swing open.

As Alicia and Choice sit outside their significant other jobs waiting on their mates to get off work, the double doors swings, it was just Samantha's boss and another one of his workers. So, Choice and Alicia start asking him questions, but not before greeting him.

"Choice, Alicia, how are you guys doing and how may I help you, is everything okay?" Mr. Reynolds asks.

"Yes, Mr. Reynolds everything's fine." Alicia says.

"Yes, everything is good sir, how is everything going? Choice says.

"Business is good, I can't complain."

"Is there any chance Samantha still in there?"

Mr. Reynolds looks back to see his co-worker coming out.

"Actually, I let her go home early today, she said she wasn't feeling good, told me it was a woman's thing, and I would not understand."

Choice smiles and looks shocked at the same time.

"Well, is Adam still in there?"

"I had him go to the other facility to do some training, is everything okay with you guys?" Mr. Reynolds asks.

"Yes, everything is fine." As they look at each other and smile.

"Okay, y'all have a nice night, good night." Miss Slayer says as she walks towards her car and gets in.

Alicia looks lost and Choice looks confused as they walk to their vehicles.

"Wait a minute I don't understand, if he was doing training today how come I wasn't informed."

"Funny because she was fine when she left the house this morning."

They stare at each other for about 10 seconds, before going their separate directions but as Alicia is pulling off, she sees something weird while leaving the parking lot. She backs her car up a tad bit, and she sights a car with the license plate that reads (S.A.M.) in the back parking lot of the job, which is funny because Sam is short for Samantha.

She sat there for about 35 seconds before it registered, then she called Choice.

"What's up Alicia?"

"Choice I have a question I want to ask you."

"What's up?"

"What is your girlfriend's name?"

"Lol, Samantha, and why you ask?"

"Okay, and what kind of car does she drive?"

"Maxima, the one where the body style changed."

"And does the plates read S.A.M."

"Yea, wait what the hell."

"Let me call you right back."

"Why, wait what is going on."

"I am going to call you back, give me a minute."

"Okay hurry up because this shit is crazy."

So, Choice calls Samantha's phone and it rings four times then goes to voicemail, he calls again, it does the same thing, rings four times then it goes to voicemail. Meanwhile, Alicia drives closer to the car with the S.A.M. license plates to make sure no one is in the car, but she meets no one in it.

So, Alicia calls Adam and his phone accidentally responds because it didn't even ring, then she hears a woman on the other end say.

"Stop, before you make me bite you."

Then the phone hangs up. She looks shocked and tries to call him again, but it goes straight to voicemail this time.

Samantha calls Choice back, but his phone is in vibration mode so he did not hear it or even feel it, but it goes to voicemail and she leaves him a message. As he drives a little farther, his phone falls between the seats and as soon as he wants to make a call he begins looking for his phone, so he turns the radio off to listen for it, then his voicemail notification goes off, he grabs his phone, opens it to listen to the voicemail and after he hears it, he did a U-turn in the middle of the street.

Adam finally decides to call Alicia back.

So, 15 minutes pass by before Choice makes a U-turn in the middle of the street because of the voicemail and he has a GPS on Samantha's car, so he turns it on. And it directs him to the parking lot of her job. So, he decides to park in the dark part of the parking lot in the back, so he could not be seen and waits for her to come back. So, after one hour and fifteen minutes he sees a car pull up next to her car and she gets out and says, "Thanks a lot, I really appreciate this." Comes to find out it is her ex Dex that drops her off. Choice contemplates getting out and confronting the both of them, but he just sits there wondering why she would do this to him and fuck up their relationship. So, he decides to text her, she replies after 5 minutes.

"Where are you?"

"On my way home, what's up?"

"Nothing just checking on you I will call you back in a little while."

"Wait, you not concerned about my well-being."

"I am, but I will call you in a minute and we will talk about that too."

"Okay."

Then he calls Alicia to ask her what was up with all the questions about earlier.

"What's good Choice?"

"You tell me, can you talk?"

"Yea, what's up?"

"Okay, now I know what was up with all the questions earlier about my lady and her license plates."

"Aw, really?"

"Yea, just seen her get out the car with her ex, and I'm like what the fuck, but I'm not going to say anything I am going to keep that one in the holster."

"Oh damn, that's fucked up but that wasn't the reason I was asking you those questions, I was asking you that because I was told that she was with my husband and she was being dropped off at her car by him. But I can't tell you who told me all that information."

"I'm not asking you to tell me who told you I'm just telling you what I just saw."

"But damn if she is fucking all three of y'all, she a fukking savage."

"Wait, hold up wait a minute, so I thought she was fucking her ex and I had an idea she could be fucking your husband as well, now you think she is fucking me, your husband, and her ex." Choice says in shock.

"Think is an understatement because my woman's intuition is telling me something different."

"So, what are you saying?"

"I will show you better than I can tell you."

When Alicia sees Samantha's car, she didn't leave she just sits back in her car and goes to park far in the back where she can see and get to her car when she comes back. She turns her lights off, and she sees Samantha getting of Dex's car but to her surprise because she isn't with her husband like she thinks she was. she shakes her head and notice Choice car in the cut to her left after he turns his interior light off when he sees the car Dex is driving pull up.

So, when Adam finally calls Alicia back shit gets crazy because of what Alicia heard when she called his phone.

"Hello, babes." Alicia says.

"What's up, honey?"

"I don't know, but don't make me bite you." Alicia says with sarcasm.

"I mean you can if you want to." Adam says while laughing.

"Oh really, so did she bite you?" Alicia asks.

"Who and what you are talking about?"

"I don't know maybe the chick that I heard in the background when I called you and someone picked up and I let it play for like 5 min before it hung up."

"Whatever stop playing, anyway what's up crazy."

"I don't know you tell me playa, playa you been a busy man I see, but when did you know you was doing training at the other facility and when were you going to tell me you were leaving work early to go there."

"Mr. Reynolds asked me at the last minute, and I didn't get a chance to tell you because my phone died, and by the time I put it on the charger it didn't charge that much before I left work, then I put it on the charger in the car and accidentally left it in the car when I went in the building."

"Oh, so when your phone finally charged, you couldn't text me, and for the record, you do know I came to your job right?"

"It was in the car the whole time and I am sorry baby."

"It's cool, what are you doing now?"

"Heading home."

"Okay, I will see you when you get here."

"Okay baby, sorry again."

"Okay, but you still need to explain who was going to bite you."

"I guess and okay I will when I see you in a little while."

"Okay."

So, Samantha calls Choice back, and he answers but he is on a call with Alicia and the two of them are talking all kinds of freaky shit then Samantha's call drops but she calls him back and he tells Alicia to hold on for a second and clicks over. Samantha ask him to bring something to eat and something to drank, he says okay and clicks back over to finish talking to Alicia and while continuing the nasty talk, saying what he wants to do to her, how he loves how she smells, and how she makes him feel when he around her and out of nowhere a voice said I wish I were her; it was Samantha.

"Well, hello and where have you been miss lady." Choice says.

"Was about to ask you the same thing." Samantha says.

"I thought you had to work late, so I called myself coming up to your job to meet you at work so we could go get a bite to eat, but when I came to your job you were not there.

"I know, I tried calling you 3 times because I was having some bad cramps and I needed a ride home because they were too bad to drive, but you didn't answer. That is when I called the ambulance, called you again and it went to the voicemail."

"So, that's when I received the message and did a U-turn in the middle of the street, and rushed to Wellborn hospital but by the time I got there, they had already released you."

"I kind of had idea that when you did not answer you was still at work, then I saw Dex there at the hospital and I didn't even know he worked there. He was getting off and he gave me a ride to my car, they thought it was gas, but it was not, so they gave me a pregnancy test."

"What was the result?"

"We will talk about it when you get home."

"Okay cool." He says as he walks into the house.

"So, what were the results?" Choice asks as Samantha laughs, smiles, and kisses him.

So, Adam walks into the house to see Alicia sitting on the couch with her legs open and her hands on her knees bobbing her head with a glass of wine in hand and the rest of the bottle sitting on the floor next to her foot, she lifts her head as he drops his keys on the counter.

"What's up playboy?"

"Playboy, lmao." Adam says as he laughs and takes off his jacket

"What were you doing that you couldn't answer my phone call?"

"Good question slicker than me."

"So, what the fuck was you doing to make a motherfukker say don't make me bite you, Adam." Alicia says in rage.

"Well, that depends on what you heard." Adam says as he sits in the chair at the kitchen table before Alicia got up off the couch, put her glass down and walks up on him and got in his face.

"Don't get smart got dammit."

Adam gets up, moves her out his way then goes to sit on the couch because she's tipsy as hell and when she gets like that, she gets extremely aggressive.

"What the fuck you mean what I heard, motherfukker I just told you what I heard got dammit, don't fucking play with me dude."

"Exactly what I said, and exactly what did you hear?"

"I heard a bitch say don't make me bite you." Alicia says as she walks to get in his face and stood over him with her hands on her waist while waiting on his response.

Adam stands up, walks away again, and laughs.

Alicia gets mad as hell as she stares at him as he walks away from her. Her phone rings as he is walking away, she looks at it to see it is Choice, and then Adam grabs the phone out of her hand.

After he grabs her phone, looks at the number and laughs, and then says to her.

"You might want to answer that." Adam says as he gives back her phone.

"I'm not going to because we are talking."

"Okay, that was a good answer, you fukking cheater." Adam says as he sips his water and leans on the counter

"Whatever dude."

"That number looks familiar, was that the guy you met at the motel probably and the same dude you are still fucking because you knew I was cheating."

Alicia walks over to Adam and grabs his hand.

"Baby, wait where is your wedding ring I mean where did you lose it at." Alicia says as she drops his hand down and walks off.

Adam looks at his hand and sees it is not on his finger.

"Okay, Alicia let's put it all on the table, tonight."

Alicia stops and turns around in shock.

"Okay, but everything means everything."

"Yes, and everything not holding nothing back, and don't be shocked or surprised with my answers.

"But please respect my truth and honesty."

"Ok, I will."

"So tonight, I will cook, and we will talk."

"Okay, about to make a couple of runs and I'll see you later tonight."

"Okay."

Meanwhile, Samantha still hasn't let Choice know about the status of the results of the pregnancy test. And Choice wants to tell her how he knows she is fucking Adam which leads him to fucking Alicia. Then Alicia tells Choice that Samantha fucked her husband, so she's going to fuck her man and she's going to fuck him better than her, and she is going to do some extra freaky shit.

PART 5

Believe nothing you hear and

half of what you see

So, Samantha tells Choice that she is not pregnant, and the doctor says that she has high blood pressure and it's causing her to be dehydrated a lot and stress is part of the reason why she is feeling weak and losing breath every now and again. Which causes her to feel dizzy when she walks too long or when she sits down too long. So, they both were tired after that deep and long conversation, so they called it a night and would finish talking tomorrow over breakfast.

The smell of bacon, grits, eggs, and toast plus the sound of neo-soul music woke Samantha out of her sleep. She swung her arm over to his side of the bed to find out he wasn't there, so she gets up washes her face, brushes her teeth, and heads to the kitchen and see Choice cooking with nothing but boxers on, he senses her behind him then he turns around.

"Good morning honey, how did you sleep?" Choice asks.

"Good morning sexy and it was okay, I tossed and turned all night but eventually I went to sleep," Samantha replied.

"Yea I kind of noticed the tossing and turning cause of the way you were moving in your sleep, so is now a good time for us to finish the conversation from last night."

"It's cool, I do not mind."

So, Choice brings their plates to the table and then goes to get the orange juice, and while Samantha is putting salt and pepper on her grits, and jelly on her toast Choice starts the conversation.

"First of all, is there anything you are willing to tell me before I start asking questions." Choice asked Samantha.

"Yes, everything that happened was not all my fault and this relationship is not a one-way street. Every action deserves a reaction so everything that happened was because of something else that made me do whatever I did at that time."

"Okay, let me get this correct you have high blood pressure because of me, you are cheating on me with a married man, and you are still fucking your ex-boyfriend, wtf Sam like really."

"Yes, for all three, but you must understand something, the way you treat me is not the greatest and I know I don't treat you the best, but I have been going through a lot of stuff and you don't have time to talk to me like you use to, and you have not been there for me like you should have lately," Samantha says as she gets teary-eyed.

"Okay, let me guess, I work 60 plus hours a week, I get your hair done every other week, manicure and pedicure whenever you feel it's needed, we have dinner every Wednesday at the restaurant of your choice and breakfast every Friday, and with all that time, you couldn't find the time to talk to me?" Choice says as he puts butter on his toast, he gets up and walks to the fridge to get more ice for his drink. Samantha wipes her face as he makes his way back to the table.

"Choice you don't understand that I need you, more and more every day but you have been distant a lot lately, and that's not good or healthy for me."

"Need my ass save that fuckery for Dex or that married nigger because what you are selling, I ain't buying, and by the way did you even know he was married." Choice says in rage

"Not until."

"Until what."

"I found his ID and wedding ring."

"Wow, lmao in the same closet where your red scarf with the initials S.A.M. was found, you know the one I bought you for your birthday." Choice says while giggling.

"Wait a minute, how did you know where my scarf was at," Samantha says as she giggles.

"Let's just say I know his wife and I knew he was married." Choice says as he pours himself more orange juice.

As soon as he finishes his statement, his phone rings and it is from an 815 number that he isn't familiar with, but his neighbor's boss tells him that he is going to give his son his number because Choice works on cars, so he could call him and get his location because he needs help. He answers the call.

"Hello."

"Hey, this is Mr. Reynold's son and my dad's neighbor told me to call you because you work on cars and I needed someone to come look at my car, it stopped and was smoking."

"Aw okay, what's up, what you need my assistant with, and what's your location?"

"Off 2nd and Broadway in front of Sam's club."

"Okay, I'm about to head to work anyway so give me about 15-20 minutes I will be heading that way."

"Okay, thanks a lot I owe you one."

"It's all good."

"Did you hear anything I just said?" Samantha ask.

"Yes, I did, and it sounds like you are playing the blame game and shit I' m not trying to hear that bullshit, because it sounds like you are trying to rectify shit."

"Are you fukking serious?"

"Yes, I am." Choice says as he finishes his food, gets up in anger and gets ready for work.

"So, you are going to just get up like that in the middle of our conversation."

"I'm done talking." Choice says as he goes into the bedroom to dress as Samantha sits at the kitchen table looking confused as she finishes eating her food.

Adam and Alicia finish their conversation, well at least she thinks they did. Then Adam leaves the house to finish up some errands, and Alicia texts Choice.

Mr. Reynolds son text him to see if he is on his way, he says he'd be there in 15 minutes.

Choice makes it to Mr. Reynold's son and notices his car is still smoking.

"Damn fam what happened, by the way, I'm Choice." Choice says as he reaches out his hand.

"What's up, I'm Dexter." As Dex does the same.

"What's happening, how long your car been smoking?"

"It just started doing that when I turned the corner from leaving the gas station up the street."

Choice eyebrows raise but brush off the fact that his name was Dexter (that's Dex for short).

"Do you have antifreeze and oil in the car because that could be the reason it's smoking if one of them is empty."

"I just got an oil change the other day but I'm not sure about the antifreeze though."

"Okay, so let's check the antifreeze, yea you don't have any in here, hold up I should have some in my trunk."

So, Choice goes to get some antifreeze out of his trunk, but at the same time his name being Dex is still on his mind, but he brushes that off and goes back to Dex car and begin to pour in the antifreeze while making small talk about the car smoking.

"Have your car ever done this before?"

"Smoking no, stopped yes."

"And what was the reason it stopped before?"

"My gas gauge was broken before I got it fixed, but now it's working fine, so that shouldn't be the reason it stopped plus I have a full tank of gas."

"Okay, let me see something."

Choice gets in Dex's car and tries to start up, it acts like it wants to start but won't turn over, but the interior lights blink when he tries to start it.

"I think it's your battery, when was the last time you changed the battery."

"I just got a battery last week." Dex says as he puts his hand on his face.

Choice looks at the battery and notices a lot of corrosion around the positive and negative post on the battery.

"Was it a new battery or a used battery."

"It was a used battery."

"Okay, well that's the problem, the battery you bought was a battery that had bad cells, but they didn't tell you that, and did you get a warranty for it?"

"Yes, they gave me a 30-day warranty, so I can go back switch it out and get a Brand new one right?"

"Well, that's what you are going to have to do, but I can give you a jump that will get you to the store where you purchased the battery from."

"Okay, thanks a lot I would appreciate that."

Choice goes to get his jumping cables so he could give him a jump and comes back and continues the conversation that they were having.

"If you don't mind me asking, where were you heading to."

"I was about to meet up with a female friend of mine, but I called her, and she didn't answer so I was heading home now."

"Aw okay cool, a friend huh." Choice says as he looks up at Dex and laughs and tightens up his cables.

"Are y'all in a relationship or just fukk buddies."

"We were in a relationship but not anymore."

"Oh, damn what happened?"

"She wasn't ready for a marriage, she just wanted a relationship, so we went our separate ways because we saw life from two different perspectives."

"Aw damn, I feel you on that because it's usually the other way around."

Dex phone rings, it is the female friend calling him, so he steps away to answer.

"Hello." Dex says.

"What's happening?" Friend says.

"So, when can I see you?"

"Idk maybe later today."

"Okay well hit me and let me know if that's possible."

"Okay, I got you."

"Damn we just spoke her up, y'all still talk and fukk around." Choice says.

"Yes, every now and again or whenever we have time, but not as much as we use to." Dex says.

"Oh, really when was the last time you seen her."

"About two weeks ago."

"Okay try to start it up now."

"The interior light is bright but, it still won't turn over." Dex says.

"Okay, that means it is the battery and it needs some more juice."

Then Choice gets a text from Samantha, he looks at it but doesn't reply but Dex looks over at his phone when he takes it out and sees the number, and his eyes get big because Samantha has had the same number for over ten years.

Then Alicia calls Choice.

"What's up punk?" Alicia says.

"What's good Alicia." Choice says.

"What are you doing tonight?"

"Idk, it depends."

"Depends on what?"

"What time I get off, why what you got going on?"

"Well, I and a couple of my girls are going to have some drinks and I wanted to know if you wanted to come since Adam is going out of town tonight and he can't join us."

"It's cool where at and what time?"

"At high times around 9:30."

"Okay cool, let me see what time we are closing tonight because we are having a 1-day sale today and it can get crazy in here when these sales come around, but I'll keep you posted."

"Okay cool and don't forget silly, because I want you to hang out with us."

"I got you."

"Okay, so I will see you later then?"

"Lol, maybe."

"Whatever okay ttyl."

So, Choice finishes helping Dex with his car, had it up and running, and heads out to take care of what he intends doing. Dex's car breaks down in front of Sam's Club store and Choice goes to help Dex. And after helping him, he starts heading to work when he sees another guy having car troubles so he asks him if he was alright, the guy asks if he happens to have some jumping cables; it is going to be a great help. So, Choice pulls over and goes in his trunk to get his cables again, but as he is walking past the guy's car, he notices a box on the back-driver seat that reads, TO MY BABY Sam from Adam. He keeps walking, and thinking about all that just happen and thinks his first old buddy name is Dex which can be short for Dexter and now I see this box on his front seat that says to my baby Samantha from Adam, he is startled but continues to help him. So afterward, Choice returns and introduces himself.

"I'm sorry bro I'm Adam." Guy says.

"I'm Choice." Choice says.

"You work around here."

"Yea at Sam's club right over there."

"Really, that's crazy." Choice says as he starts smiling.

"Why you say that?" Adam says.

"No reason." Choice says.

"Aw okay, so what seems to be the problem?"

"I haven't the slightest idea, all I did was pull over to get a bottled water, turn the car off, and now it won't start back up."

"Aw okay."

"But I think it has something to do with the alarm system."

"Well go and get the manual so I can call them to see, how to disable it."

"Okay, I got you." Adam says as he goes and gets the manual.

"Here we go." Choice says as he looks for his phone.

"You, good."

"Looking for my phone."

"You can use mine."

It is part of the setup, he needs to make sure he isn't tweaking, so he dials the first three numbers of Samantha's phone number, and to his surprise, her name is one of the names that pop up and they were talking earlier that day, for about 15 minutes. He knows where he left his phone but he still calls the warranty company so it will not be obvious. Then before he had a chance to give him back his phone, a message comes through from Samantha, he grins and gives him back his phone. Then Dex sees them up the street so he pulls over to make sure they are good.

"They said I have to reset it that's all."

"What the hell, I guess."

Then Samantha text Choice while he is resetting his alarm.

"So, you are not going to tell me where you getting all this information from." Samantha asks.

He doesn't reply, so she texts him again.

"So now you not going to reply, that's what we on okay cool."

After Choice makes it back to his car to get his phone and he starts laughing after seeing the messages from Samantha and then replies.

"Now why would I tell you where I get my information, I'm crazy, but I am not that crazy." Choice replies as he starts laughing.

She thinks he is trying to play her, so she didn't reply to his message.

You see, Samantha and Choice met each other at Sam's club store, the same one he still works at now. Samantha asks for a transfer, so she now works at Sam's Club warehouse which, is about 20 minutes from Sam's club store by where Dex's car broke down at. Choice calls Samantha back.

"What's up?"

"What's up little crazy?"

"Aw, now you want to call me."

"Shut yo ass up, but what's up with these messages you been sending me."

"I was just asking you a question and I thought you were ignoring me or didn't want to answer."

"No, it wasn't like that, I left my phone in the car."

"So are you going to answer the questions or not."

"Yea, give me a second, I'm over here by your job right now helping these guys that had car trouble. where you at?"

"On my way to work."

"Okay if I am finished by the time you get this way, I will wait on you and I will answer all your questions we talked about earlier in person, are you close?"

"Okay cool, is this your car parked on the side of the green Lexus?"

"Yea."

"Behind the black Tahoe."

"Yea."

"Okay, here I come."

While Choice is leaving from helping Dex, he sees Adam, so he pulls over to assist him with his car and while he is helping Adam, Dex sees them and pulls over to make sure they are okay. Then Alicia calls Choice to let him know that the place they are going to tonight has been changed. And the funny thing is Adam use to have the same ringtone for her that Choice have now (lovers and friends by usher), Adam looks at his phone thinking it is his wife calling, but it is not, it is Choice phone ringing.

Choice sees her calling, but he sends her to the voicemail because he is assisting Adam, then he starts laughing.

Adam looks shocked because it is funny how his wife's old ringtone is now Choice present ringtone, but he plays it cool until he gets more info out of the situation as Dex pulls up.

"Hey, y'all good?" Dex says.

"Aw what's good Dex yea we cool, I just needed a jump, that's all." Adam says.

"What's good?" Choice says.

Dex shakes Choice's hand.

"Seems like everybody having car trouble today I see, but why all of us is here I have a question for you guys." Dex asks.

"What's up fam?" Adam says as he looks at Dex

"We listening." Choice says as he leans on Adam's car.

"Okay, I've always wondered, what's the deal with giving a woman her own ringtone."

"Honestly, I've given my wife some freaky ringtones, because it gets me ready for her before I even get to her and anticipates what I want to do to her when I finally see her." Adam says.

"I feel you on that one because my girl has had a couple of ringtones depending on what kind of history the song holds, lol." Choice says.

"Okay, can you give more than one woman the same ringtone?" Dex asks.

"Technically, you can but you shouldn't, because every woman should serve their own purpose for that specific ringtone." Adam says.

"I agree with that because it had to mean something when they were assigned that ringtone in the first place." Choice says.

And at that moment Dex phone rings, his ringtone is (Same girl by R-Kelly and Usher) it is Samantha. Adam looks at him grins and Choice looks and laughs, as Dex looks, smiles and answers, and walks off to talk.

"Where you at?"

"Sam's club on Broadview, assisting some guys with car troubles."

"Aw okay, You good?"

"Yea I'm always good, are you alright?"

"Yes, was just checking on you, but alright I'm going to hit you back in a minute." Samantha says as she sits and thinks.

"Okay."

Then he hangs up and looks at the phone and says in his head, this is weird, and he knows Samantha sneaky ass plus that was suspicious as hell but thinks nothing of it and goes back to where Adam and Choice are at by Choice's car.

Then Samantha sends Choice a message.

"Honey I just started bleeding, and I am heading back home, I need you asap."

"Okay, I'm omw right now."

So, Choice tells the fellas if everybody's car is good; he needs to go because he has an emergency that he must attend to now. So, he gets in his car and speeds off down the road, shortly after that Adam leaves, then Samantha direct messages him and tells him to call her asap.

Now, Adam is on his way to work but he can't get over the fact that Samantha's picture pops up when she calls, Dex and Alicia name pops up when she calls Choice and this has him wondering what kind of bullshit is really going on.

1st Samantha tells Dex she is going to call him back. But she never leaves from where she is parked because when she sees the three of them together by her job, she pulls over, parks and sits in the cut and watch her plan work its magic. 2nd she tells Choice that she is bleeding, so he can rush home to her side, 3rd she direct messaged Adam to call her asap, he calls, she tells him she is running late from work because she is having car troubles, lol.

She watches Choice speed off to make his way to her because he thinks she is at home, she looks at Dex as he lets his car run for a little while before he leaves, and gets Adam's attention by telling him she will be late as she is having car trouble. But the only problem is that Choice didn't leave, he drives up the street and around the corner, he feels something fishy is going on, so he turns Samantha GPS on to see if she is really on her way home and it shows she is three minutes from where he is, he rubs his chin and says, "oh really." So, he drives around the block and stops at the stop sign and sees her car some hundred feet ahead, and the license plates read S.A.M, he laughs. He parks back far away so she can't see his car, then Adam replies to Samantha.

"Okay, I'll see you when you get here."

He doesn't feel anything fishy, so he heads to work. Then Choice calls Samantha's phone.

"What up dude?" Samantha says.

"What are you doing?" Choice asks.

"Sitting here not feeling good."

"Sitting where?"

"In my car."

"Aw okay well you need a car wash."

"Huh, well what that supposed to mean." Samantha says as she looks around.

Then Choice walks up to her car and she is speechless and shocked.

"I guess the bleeding stopped huh."

Samantha laughs, giggles, and laughs again.

"Wow." Samantha says as she smiles.

"So how long have you been sitting here?"

"Not that long."

"Now you really think I believe that bullshit."

"I don't know what you believe, you asked me, and I told you."

"Okay, so you going to just sit here and watch all this play out, your boyfriend, ex-boyfriend, and your side dude working together."

"Look dude I can explain."

"No need, you good I already know what's up."

"Really dude."

"Yea you don't have to."

While driving for about 10 minutes then he sees Choice down the street and pulls up on him, while he is talking.

Then Mr. Reynolds calls Adam and tells him he needs him to stop at Sam's club store to pick up some invoice papers from their last delivery, he says okay. But on his way, he sees Choice leaning over in Samantha's driver car window. So, he goes over there.

So, it's something that Alicia and Samantha don't know. You see every Sunday the three of them play basketball and talk shit. But they don't actually know each other just know of each other. So, one day after a hoop session they are talking with some other guys and they make a bet amongst each other. Choice says he bets he can fuck a married woman, more than once. So, Dex and Adam take the bet. Then Dex bet that he can fuck an ex after she gets in a committed relationship. Adam and Choice take the bet. And then, Adam bet he can fuck a co-worker at work during their shift, Dex and Choice take the bet. They all agree and confirm it.

Meanwhile, Alicia plots on Choice because she finds out Samantha is fucking him, and she knows Adam works with her. And while driving Alicia sees Adam drive pass her, she makes a U-turn and follows him, he sees her and pulls over as she pulls up on the side of him.

"Where you headed?" Alicia says.

"Up there to holler at Choice, follow me." Adam says.

"Fosho."

So, the two of them pull up on Samantha and Choice as the two of them look at each other as they are pulling up right after Dex makes it to them.

"Wow, this is crazy ass hell." Dex says.

"Who you telling?" Choice says.

"OMFG!" Samantha says as she gets out of her car.

"Adam what the hell you are doing over here?" Alicia says.

"Heading to the warehouse to pick up some invoices, but the real question is how long you been fukking Choice." Adam says as Samantha looks at Choice and smiles.

Alicia looks stunned and shocked.

"Well damn Alicia." Samantha says as Choice turns and looks at Alicia and smiles.

"And I want to know why Samantha was sitting over here watching us." Choice says as he looks at Samantha and she laughs and grins.

"Wait a minute, hold the fuck up."

"Y'all are funny as hell." Dex says while laughing as everyone looks around at each other and laughs.

"Not as funny as how you were getting in your feelings about Samantha, so bad that you started missing what the two of y'all had when y'all was together, you fucked around and started catching feelings again lmao." Choice says while smiling.

"Whoa, wtf going on?" Samantha says.

"Damn Samantha bitch really, lol." Alicia says.

Choice starts laughing.

"Wait a minute, so Alicia you knew I was fucking your husband?" Samantha asks her.

"Yea what other reason would I need to fuck Choice." Alicia says as she leans on her car.

"And Choice you knew I was fucking Adam and used to fuck Dex?" Samantha asks Choice.

"Yes, I knew because we setup dates when everything was going to happen in this little situation we have here, lol." Choice says.

"Oh, yea Alicia don't worry about what you are thinking about I already know what it is." Adam says.

"So, wait y'all sneaky asses plotted on us." Alicia says as she folds her arms.

All the guys start laughing.

"You see here is how we made this plan work," but before he can tell how it happened, Alicia and Samantha start laughing at the same time loud as hell while the fellas are in the middle of their joke.

"So, men really think they are sneaker than women huh Sam." Alicia says as she looks at Samantha and laughs.

"They do, but before y'all give us the scoop on how y'all did it, let us break it down how men react from women actions." Samantha says as the guys stop laughing and look at each other.

"What the hell they are talking about?" Dex says.

"Yea what are y'all asses talking about now." Adam says.

"Yea I want to hear this bullshit." Choice says

"Okay but first, Samantha and I met way before she and Choice got together, I met her 5 years before she and Dex started dating" Alicia says.

"Not to mention we have had the same beautician for 10 years." Samantha says as she goes over and sits on Alicia's car as Alicia stands next to her and folds her arms smiling and giggling.

"Everything you guys did, was done because we wanted y'all to do it not because y'all thought y'all was being slick." Alicia says while laughing.

Dex looks at Adam and Adam looks at Choice as he looks at Dex as Choice puts his hands in his pocket.

"How do y'all think I met Dex." Samantha says as all three of them look crazy, lost, and confused.

Choice looks shocked, pissed, mad, angry, etc.

"Aw don't look mad boo boo it's okay, but anyway that car you were driving about a year ago, Mr. Reynolds sold it to me." Alicia says while looking at Adam.

Adam bites his bottom lip in anger.

"If y'all didn't know you see Dex dad use to have a car dealership, and for the record, he cosigned for my car, yea the same one you made the payments on faithfully, Adam." Alicia says while grinning.

"Are you fucking serious, now it's making sense, wow gtfoh." Adam says.

"You got to be fucking kidding me!" Dex says while frowning.

Alicia looks at Dex in disgust.

"Wait Samantha, what this nigga Dex over there laughing at?" Alicia says while laughing.

"So Dex you want to tell them, what you didn't tell them, or should I show them the texts that I received?" Samantha says.

"Yea Sam, it would be better and funnier if you tell and show them." Alicia says and she leans on the car.

"You know what, that sounds like a plan." Samantha says.

So Dex is being eyeballed and evil-eyed by Adam, googled eye by Sam, laughed at by Alicia, and starred at by Choice.

Then Adam looks at Alicia.

"So, Alicia you decided to invited Choice to hangout tonight because you knew I was going out of town huh, Alicia." Adam says.

Alicia puts her head down, Choice grins, Dex giggles, Samantha smiles, and Adam smirks.

"Wait, hold up, she invited Choice to the place that we usually hang out at, and wait a minute Adam we work together, and you didn't even tell me you were going out of town." Samantha says while smiling.

"I told your ass never to get hooked on a dick that belongs to another woman, just because y'all fucking doesn't mean y'all friends." Alicia says while giggling.

"Let's stop right there and nip this in a bud. How about we all meet up at the spot later on tonight before Adam catches his flight and just put everything on the table." Dex says.

Everyone looks at each other and smiles then giggles.

"I'm feeling that and I'm just going to change my flight, fukk the bullshit," Adam says.

"Okay, that sounds fun and interesting," Samantha says as she smiles.

"That's what I'm talking about." Alicia says while laughing.

"Yea let's get to the bottom of all this fuckery." Samantha says.

"I'm game let's do it." Alicia says.

"I'm down and this is going to be fun." Dex says.

"Okay fukk it, let's make it happen." Choice says while laughing.

"I'm down." Samantha says.

So, everybody agrees and gets in their cars and go about their day, Dex text Samantha, Alicia text Adam, Samantha text Choice and Adam sees a message from Samantha, while Choice text Alicia.

Samantha doesn't respond to Dex's message, but she calls him.

"Hello." Dex says while laughing.

"What the fuck you on dude, yo ass tripping." Samantha says.

"Don't be calling my phone talking shit, the hell wrong with you." Dex says.

"Nigga you are doing too much, and yo ass need to chill the fukk out before this shit gets out of hand." Samantha says.

"Whatever, and you haven't seen shit yet." Dex says as he laughs.

"What the fukk?" Samantha says.

"I got some shit up my sleeve, so be careful of what you say and do." Dex says.

"Yea well if that's what you on don't forget it's a two-way street asshole." Samantha says as she hangs up the phone.

Adam doesn't reply to Alicia's text, he just calls her.

"Hello." Alicia says.

"You been a busy lady I see." Adam says.

"Not as busy as your ass." Alicia says as she giggles.

"Yea I'm going to need to change my flight in the morning because I don't want to miss this night, it is going to be one to remember."

"That makes two of us because I think you got a fatal attraction on your hands."

"She just like my third leg lmao."

"I can believe that too, but you like her wet, wet, so stop fronting dude." Alicia says while laughing as Adam smiles.

"Lmao but let me change this flight, I will see you later."

Then Choice messages Alicia and tells her he wants to see her before they hang out with everyone tonight.

"Tonight, your ass going to have to make a Choice lol." Adam says.

"Yea aight, that's what I'm not going to have to do because your ass stuck with me until death do us part, so whatever, but I will see you later." Alicia says.

"Damn cocky and confident, I love that shit, and okay."

And Alicia finally replies to Choice's message.

"I'm done I can't do this no more, it's been fun, but it was fun while it lasted." Alicia says.

"Are you sure?" Choice asks.

"Yes and no, it's a slippery slope lol."

"I guess, so is that a yes."

"I'll let you know, give me like an hour."

"Okay cool."

Then Choice texts Sam after he texts Alicia, and Adam sees a text from Samantha.

"You going to make it your business to see me before we all link up tonight, huh." Samantha says.

"Hell yea, what you got in mind." Adam says.

"That dick."

"Yea I can come disrespect that pussy, hit me when you on your way to the spot."

"Will do."

Alicia replies to Choice text.

"Wow." Alicia says.

"I know right this is going to be weird as hell tonight." Choice replies with laughing emoji.

"Who you telling, you better hope I don't take your ass down in the washroom when we get there."

"Lol, and how are you going to pull that off?"

"Let me worry about that, plus I know all Adam passwords to all his electronic devices, and he is planning on hitting your girl before we go out tonight anyway."

"Are you fucking serious, wow."

"I know right, and I thought we be on bullshit they on the same kind of bullshit, lol."

"I see, and I guess we on then."

"Hit you when I'm on my way to the location."

"Aight bet."

So, everybody heads home to get ready for tonight.

Choice walks in the house and hears Samantha in the shower because she needs to clean up after her and Adam's sex session in her car, so he gets in the shower with her and makes her cum two times from the head and three times from the dick. Meanwhile, on the other side of town, Alicia is seen getting out of her car walking funny with the Bambi legs because Choice knocks some of her screws loose. And Alicia goes home and washes up because Choice made her cum four times from straight dick. Meanwhile, everyone else gets ready and on their way to the spot, that they all agreed on.

Part 6

Let the games begin

Adam and Alicia ride together, Choice and Samantha ride together, by the time they make it there was Dex already there and waves his hand to signal them where he is at, and he says first rounds on him.

So, they sit down, complement each other, and chat for a second before ordering drinks.

"How is everyone doing, what will we be having to drink?" Waiter says.

First, a bottle of Moet and I will have a top-shelf long island." Dex says.

"I'll take a blue motherfukker, with a double shot of patron," Alicia says.

"A double shot of Dusse and a Heineken." Adam says.

"A Caribbean teaser and two shots of apple crown." Samantha says.

"A Corona and a double shot of 1738." Choice says.

"Okay gotcha coming right up, can I get you all some food?"

"Y'all want some chicken?" Adam asks.

"That's cool, cause I'm hungry as hell." Samantha says.

"Do yall have garlic parmesan?" Choice asks waiter.

"Yes, we have garlic parmesan, buffalo, original, honey barb-e-que, hot BBQ, spicy garlic, a whole lot more on the back of the menu."

"We'll just take 25 honey BBQ, 40 buffalo plus a pan of fries." Adam says.

"Okay, going to go put that in but will be right back with those drinks."

"Samantha how long you and Choice been together?" Adam asks.

"About a year and a half." Samantha says.

"Are you guys planning on getting married?" Adam says.

Alicia coughs and says gtfoh.

"Really bitch." Samantha says after looking at her and rolling her eyes.

Alicia laughs and smiles

"What I was just sneezing." Alicia says.

"So, Alicia how the job coming along." Dex asks her.

"No complaints I mean it's a job." Alicia says.

"So Dex whatever happened with you and Samantha?"

As the waiter brings their drinks, and Samantha takes one of the shots of the crown and takes a sip of her drink after hearing the question.

Dex laughs and replies.

"The same thing that's going to happen once you realize it's not you, it's her." Dex says as he starts laughing.

Adam spits out beer.

"Wow, shots fired."

Samantha looks and stares him down and speaks.

"Really nigga."

Alicia sips her Patron and looks around.

Choice looks stuck and lost all at the same time.

Dex sips his drink and laughs.

"Samantha stop looking at me like I'm a meal or something." Choice says as he licks his lip and drinks.

"Maybe I'm hungry."

"So, you want to be a teaser huh."

"Not a teaser I'm a pleaser baby after winking her eye."

"Look at these freaky fucks." Alicia says as she laughs.

So Dex sneaks and looks at Samantha out of his peripheral vision, even though Choice is tipsy, he still catches him.

"Stop that shit Dex you was not her choice I was so stop the eyeballing, and that's my last time telling you that." Choice says.

"Wait what I just miss." Samantha says.

"Dex over there on some drunk shit, and he was staring at Samantha hard as hell and Choice caught him." Alicia says as she stirs her drink before finishing it as the waiter comes back over.

"Wow he be doing too damn much, and he has had too much to drink." Samantha says.

"Yes, I noticed that soon as I came in the spot, he watched you all the way till you sat down Sam." Alicia says.

"Yea I'm not for no drama so Dex chill out fam." Choice says.

Dex sips his drink.

"Fam you don't want to go there with me, I promise you don't." Dex says.

Alicia cuts the drama off in the middle.

"Wait a minute, I thought we was all up here to have a couple of drinks and to have a good time while enjoying each other's company, y'all fucking up the mood." Alicia says.

"Me too but Dex ass tripping on some drunk shit, fukking up the mood and shit." Choice says.

"Choice just chill out, his ass is semi-drunk." Samantha says.

"I am cool that's him, and I know he tipsy because he always keeps a drink in his car." Choice says.

Dex sips his beer, smiles while looking at Choice.

"Worry about your own shit, and not mines okay dude." Dex says with frustration.

Adam gets frustrated, gets up, and tries to grab Dex to pull him to the side to talk to him but Dex yanks away.

"Naw bro come here for a second, let me holler at you." Adam says as Dex looks at him and gets up to talk to him.

"What's up with your boy Choice, he fukking up the mood." Samantha says.

"That nigga drunk, but I'm going to sober his ass up if he keeps it up." Choice says.

Sam whispers in Alicia's ear "we might have to do something about him in a little while because once he gets too drunk, he sings like a canary."

"I was just thinking the same thing, you know what I got a plan just follow my lead." Alicia says.

"Gotcha."

So, Adam and Dex are having a conversation away from the table and he tells the waiter to bring a second round for their table.

"Bro, cool out, just enjoy yourself, and let's continue to enjoy each other's company."

"I have no problem doing that but, I feel like they are fucking with me and if it happens again, I swear I'm not holding no punches fuck that." Dex says as he walks off and heads back to the table.

But Sam and Alicia are planning something to get Dex off the bullshit, but they didn't get a chance to do that.

"Oh, my fucking god! I hate a fake ass nigga and it makes me want to whoop their ass when they be on that pussy shit." Alicia says.

"Yes, I feel you 100% and it still pisses me off as well," then Dex walks in on the ass end of the conversation between Alicia and Samantha and he sits down, and they keep talking, while Adam is telling them to chill out and tone it down with a hand gesture, they didn't and that pissed Dex off because he knows they are talking about him while he is sitting right there, then he just explodes.

As the waiter brings the second round.

"Wait am I hearing things or are the two of y'all over there talking about me behind my back and while I'm sitting right here, like for real." Dex says.

"It depends if it sounds like we're talking about you, then we are." Alicia says.

"And if you don't like it then you don't have to be here." Samantha says as she smacks her lips.

"Damn why don't y'all chill out, Jesus Christ!" Adam says.

"No Adam let them get it out, it's cool." Dex says as he sips his drink.

"Well since we are talking about stuff and people let's put everything out there."

Alicia looks at Samantha as both see some bullshit in the air.

"Dex what are you saying?" Choice says.

"Saying, nigga I said it the fuck you talking about." Dex says.

"Whatever Dex do what you got to do fam I'm done." Choice says as he grabs his glass.

"Damn y'all cut it out now, y'all fucking up the mood, damn."

"Fuck that shit dawg I'm tired of the bullshit, so Sam since you want to keep talking shit did you tell Choice that you fucked Adam in his car in the job parking lot, last Friday when you drove it to work."

Sam's face drops as she looks stunned.

"No, the fuck he didn't, you got to be kidding me." Alicia screams out and looks at Adam and Dex.

"Don't look stupid now Samantha and Alicia yes, the fuck I did."

"Don't start shit you can't finish dude."

"Okay I will stop but only if you tell Adam how you really got your job, and I mean the truth."

"No, the fuck you didn't." Alicia says as she stands up and throws her drink on him, then Adam grabs her from going at Dex for what he said.

"Sam, what is he talking about?" Choice says while looking at her.

"And since I was asked not to start something I can't finish, I'm going to finish it and Choice I have not forgotten about your ass either bro, you acting like you are innocent, but you can't fool me and by the way, you have been fucking Alicia way longer than you been fucking Samantha."

Everybody looks shocked and says wow all at the same time, then Choice stands up and walks towards Dex.

"Keep on talking bitch." Choice says as he gets in Dex's face and Adam breaks them up.

"Y'all calm the fuck down and sit y'all ass down and cut that shit out."

"Fuck boy you got me fucked up because you are jumping in the wrong person's face, you need to be in Adam's face because he is the one that makes Sam's juice box drip daily and I heard she sleeps well after. while you are on the other side of town licking and sticking on Alicia every chance you get lol."

Alicia jumps up and throws a glass at him but Dex ducks it.

"You got some nerves you stupid bitch."

Adam looks at Alicia shocked and surprised.

"What the fuck Alicia?"

"Wait a minute you told me how you got the job, but I'm starting to believe it is not true, so my question to you is how you really got the job, though." Choice asks her.

"I told you how I got the job, what you don't believe me or something."

"It's not that I don't believe you, I'm just lost on how Dex come up with how he believes you got the job, versus what you told me."

"Believe nigga big facts, I know how she got the job."

Alicia moves over and sits closer to Adam.

"Honey we can discuss that at home, this not the time or place for that conversation." Alicia says as she tries to grabs his hand and he yanks away from her.

"Don't touch me until you tell me the truth."

"Are you seriously doing this right now?"

"Yes, I am."

Alicia looks shocked and looks over at Dex to see him laughing and grinning.

"It's mighty funny how you quiet now Samantha, but if you will not tell him the truth then I will tell him because I warned you earlier to leave me the fuck alone."

Alicia looks over at Dex again as he sips his drink and grins, her rage hit its peak, she grabs the Moet bottle off the table and attempts to throw it at him, but Choice grabs her arm.

"You lucky bitch, I fucking hate your ass."

"That's what you on huh, Adam can you get control of your animal homie."

"Really dude you had no right putting me on blast like that Dex, it was disrespectful and bogus as hell."

"And you had no right talking about my dad to Samantha, thinking it would stay between the two of y'all, dude she done told me all kinds of shit about your ass, but I'm going to get back to your ass as soon as I finish with these motherfukkers."

"You know for someone who can't keep a woman, you sure have a lot to say about everybody else's relationship." Choice says as he finishes his drink.

"Damn straight and I'm far from finish."

Alicia sneaks and grabs another bottle while everyone isn't paying attention and throws it at Dex's ass but this time it makes it to him but misses him by an inch.

"Whoa, you are big mad."

"Fukk you."

"Damn she almost hit his ass and she going to hit him next time."

"Ooohhh should have his stupid ass."

"Fucking bastard."

Dex looks at Alicia laughs and starts talking more shit.

"I'm not the one who had to fuck and suck my dad to get a job."

Choice looks at Dex then looks at Samantha.

Alicia puts her hands over her mouth in shock.

Adam balls up his fist in a rage because he is fed up with Dex drunk shit talking.

Samantha mumbles.

"No, this nigga didn't just say what I told him when we were drunk that night."

"Wait, what did you just mumble Sam?"

Samantha looks surprised as Choice hears her mumble what she said. Adam stands up.

"Wait hold up one fucking minute, so you mean to tell me that you fukked my boss, what the fuck Alicia and you call me sneaky you got to be kidding me." Adam says in anger.

"Honey, let me explain." As she starts crying and tries to grab his hand, but he yanks away from her.

"You can get the fuck off me," as he finishes his drink and gets up from the table and goes over and knocks Dex out, "Clean the fuck out."

"Damn, you got knocked the fuck out."

"Yes, he did."

Alicia smiles with tears falling.

While Dex is on the other side getting off the floor recovering from that hit by Adam as Adam stands over him.

"You bitch ass nigga; we talk about everything else you could have told me that shit with your punk ass." Adam says as he walks away from the table where Dex lays on the floor.

Sam and Alicia try to grab Adam as he walks away but he pulls away from both, stops, and looks at Samantha.

"Samantha, nothing against you but can you leave me alone." He looks at Alicia in disgust. As Samantha looks at Alicia, she drops her head.

Part 7

Surprise, Surprise

So, Sam turns around after trying to cool Adam down to look over to see Choice looking at her with anger.

"Now we have a serious problem, because it was not your place to try and calm down her man, dumbass and two when did you have the time to tell stupid all this shit that he is mentioning."

"Bae wait."

"Don't fucking bae me, are you stupid or dumb."

"Who the fukk you talking to?"

"Yo ass."

Samantha gets quiet.

"And that was a long time ago when we were kicking it and it was not supposed to leave the two of us, but I guess I was wrong." Samantha says.

"So, what else was said that wasn't supposed to leave the two of y'all, because I was told some things that only me and you knew about, because dumbass over there was drunk and some shit slipped out."

"Omfg are you fucking serious?"

Choice smiles and giggles.

"Yea because y'all must have been really talking because he was giving me times, dates, and everything."

"Wait, he was?"

Choice looks at her and sips.

Alicia comes back to the table.

"Excuse me but Sam can I borrow you for a minute?"

Samantha stands up.

"Hold up, excuse me Alicia but no you cannot borrow her, we are here talking right now so you can go make sure your guy is okay and let me deal with her ass, now Sam sit your ass back down."

Samantha smiles sits back down, Alicia smiles and walks off.

"Now back to your unloyal ass."

So as Choice tells Samantha about herself and she listens and understands where he is coming from, and they are cool for the moment. Meanwhile, Dex is sucking on his bloody bottom lip as the waiter walks up giggling with a cup of ice and hands it to Dex.

"Here you go sir, is everything okay over here?"

"Yea, we good."

"Can we have a bottle of Elegant Flavors Chardonnay wine?"

"Okay, would you like me to bring another round back?"

Choice looks around at the table.

"Yes, that's fine."

So, Alicia and Adam comes back to the table, sits down.

Dex is still sucking on that damn ice that the waiter brought him. Choice and Sam are talking and sipping, then Alicia and Adam kick off the conversation.

"Okay, so me and this headache of mines (as Alicia slaps him in the back of the head) I mean Alicia has decided to spill it all, everything but everyone must be on board to do the same."

"Hold up Wait, everything."

"Okay, y'all mean like no holding back, no secrets, everything."

"Yup, yup, y'all down."

Samantha drinks her whole drink.

"Wheeew Okay, I'm going to need another drink for this."

"Okay, when Dex finishes sucking on that ice." Everyone laughs at the same time.

"This applies to Dex and Adam too, come all the way clean, no sugar coating and no cutting corners fuck everybody feelings." Choice says.

"Aw believe me I'm not holding back shit, but I did invite someone to join us to put a little spice on this game, therefore no one can lie about anything because this person has some truth about a lot of our situations." Adam says as everyone looks at each other.

"Who in the hell did this nigga invite?" Samantha whispers to Alicia.

"Your guess is as good as mine Sam but I am just as curious as you are."

Meanwhile, the guys are not concerned about who this guest is, they just want to get the game started.

So, everyone is at the table, and here comes Adam's guest, and it is…….

"Hello everyone." Mr. Reynolds says.

Samantha's face freezes as she smiles, Choice grins then laughs. Adam greets him with a firm handshake and Dex smiles, Alicia smiles then laughs followed by a sip of her drink, Dex smirks, then ice shoots out of his mouth, lol.

"Looks like things got a little rough over here, huh, son."

"Excuse me, waiter, can I have a pitch of Stella, a bottle of Belair," looks at Dex lip and laughs "and some more ice?" Mr. Reynolds says as he takes off his coat and sits down and gets comfortable.

"So, who going to start?" Adam asks.

"Okay, I will go first, Alicia how many of the guys sitting here at this table right now have you fucked?"

Alicia laughs, smiles, grins, and smirks as the waiter brings the next rounds of drinks.

"All of them except Dex, as she finishes her drink."

Adam's mouths drop, Choice grins and laughs, Dex laughs as he spits ice out of his mouth, Mr. Reynolds was pouring him a glass of wine until he hears that then he stops.

"Say what, say what, what you just say." He laughs

"We being honest so fuck it, it's okay for a man to fuck several women but not okay for a woman to do it, stop it."

"We not saying that but damn, Alicia you a savage."

"Yea Alicia, you fucked me up with that one as well, but I feel where you are coming from though have fun girl," as she gives her a high five.

"You feel me girl, and that's just the tip of the iceberg."

"Y'all have not heard shit wait till this drink kicks in, who going next."

"Okay, Alicia since you on a roll-out of all these guys at this table who fucked you the best, who gave the best head, who has the biggest dick, and who made you look at sex on another level, in a good way like spontaneous as hell."

"Damn nigga you did waste no time."

As all the guys laugh and poured up as Samantha sips what she has left in her glass before giving her glass to Choice so he can pour her more wine.

Alicia looks shocked because everyone is waiting on her to answer.

"Come on Alicia, let's go."

"Yea, you set the pace, Alicia."

"Okay whew, let's see Choice has the biggest dick."

Dex smiles

"Adam fucks me the best."

Adam sips his drink and smirks

"Mr. Reynolds gave the best head and made me look at sex different."

Mr. Reynolds laughs.

Then Alicia takes her glass of wine to the head and calls for the waiter to get her a double shot.

Meanwhile, Adam looks shocked, Dex laughs, Mr. Reynolds smiles and Choice laughs as well.

"Well damn hoe you never told me none of that." Samantha says in shock.

"I couldn't but if you didn't know, now you know, lol."

"Okay, my turn." Adam says as he cracks his knuckles and pours himself a glass of Stella.

"Choice my main man."

"Oh shit." Choice laughs.

"Now that I know you have fucked my wife lol. Okay so who squirts, who cremes, who gives the best head, who is the best overall freak, and who pussy is better."

Choice looks up and sighs then takes a drink and giggles.

"Mmmm okay here goes, Sam has the best pussy."

Sam laughs loud as hell, while Alicia muffs Samantha.

"Sam squirts and crèmes, but you must hit that certain spot but on the other hand Alicia is a walking faucet, she can squirt for hours. The head is a tie because orally neither has any limits they both some beast. Best overall freak is Alicia, she doesn't care where she at when she wants it, she wants it."

"My kind of freak." Mr. Reynolds mumbles.

"Really dad, did you have to say that, lmao."

"Y'all said we being honest right."

"Well damn Sam, you been doing a lot huh lol."

"Not really but I'm pretty sure you have as well," she pauses as she is about to say something.

"You know what, I'm going to save all my questions for your ass."

Adam grins and giggles while putting lemons in his water

"Okay, Samantha you ready?"

"Yea, wait," she sips her drink "okay, I'm ready, shiiit whew!"

"Have you and Mr. Reynolds ever had a sexual encounter, if so explain."

"Yes so, one day we were at work and I was helping him with a business plan he had. And he just starts telling me how he liked me, like my hair, how I come to work smelling good, and then he just starts to tell me how men should appreciate women more. And how he been liking me ever since I started working there, I started blushing, then he mumbled god damn and started to fix his pants then I noticed his dick got hard as hell and it was showing through his pants. So, I said oh wow, then he was like wow what, I'm like what are you happy about, and he was like, you. So, I started blushing again because that was cute. But as I got ready to go, he grabbed my hand, pulled me close, and kissed me. So, I said Mr. Reynolds what are you doing we can't do this, and I walked out."

Adam looks shocked.

"Old slick ass, lol."

"Pops you be on good bullshit."

"But she never said no so, I mean hey." He says as he shrugs his shoulders.

Everyone laughs then he says "okay my turn."

"So Dex have you ever fucked Alicia, if so explain." Mr. Reynolds asks.

Everyone looks patiently waiting on him to answer, while Adam sits back in his chair and lights his cigar as Dex looks at him with the evil smirk

"No, but almost, okay here's what happened, one day when I and Samantha was dating Alicia came over to the house with her."

"Omg, I knew he was going to bring that shit up."

"Oh wow."

"Just listen, you about to find out what really happened that night." Dex says as he sucks on the ice.

Dex starts laughing while looking at Alicia.

"I was in the shower when they came in and Samantha told me she was on her way over, but she never said she had someone with her. So, I heard Samantha say damn I left it in the car, so I did my usual routine and got out of the shower naked like I always do but to my surprise, Alicia was in the room on the bed when I walked in I tried to cover up but it was too late she had seen all my goods, she smiled and said damn Dex that's a nice piece of work."

Alicia starts to sip her drink a little more as he continues to tell what happened that night.

"Then she looked out the window and saw Samantha pulling off, then Samantha texted her and said running to the store she will be right back, she replied okay and put the phone down and walked over toward me moved my hands and begin given me some head while she playing with her pussy, it lasted for about 15 minutes before we heard Samantha pulls up because of her music, so I went back in the washroom and she went to sit on the couch and started playing in her phone, and that was it."

"You slut, that's why you were grinning when I walked back in the house that day."

"Hell yea."

"Well damn Dex your lucky ass."

"I swear."

So Dex spits out ice, laughs, and speaks.

"So Adam, you ready?"

"Hell, yea come on with it, let's go."

"Okay, have you ever fucked Samantha and Alicia on the same day, if so, who was the best?"

"Damn and yes, and Sam won because she made me cum two times from sex and two times from head."

Alicia looks at Sam.

"Bitch."

Samantha smiles and laughs.

"Well, I will be damned."

"I swear."

"This is getting good, shiiit so who is going to be the next victim of the tell-all, lol."

"I got this one." Samantha says as she laughs.

Choice smirks and laughs.

"Come on with it Sam."

"Have you ever been fucking me and thought another woman?"

"No, but I have thought about what it would be like to fuck you and Alicia together."

Alicia smiles.

"Oh wow."

Alicia looks at Samantha and smiles as Samantha smiles back at her.

"Okay this Stella running through me I need to take a washroom break; I'll be right back." Adam says.

So, everyone decides to take a washroom break.

"This shit getting crazy." Choice says.

"I swear." Dex says.

"Who you are you telling?" Adam says while smiling.

Meanwhile in the ladies' room.

"Sam, I believe this is about to get real, really quick with these questions that's being asked tonight."

"I was thinking the same thing."

So meanwhile they are some things discussed in the lady's washroom, that are going to make it back to the table discussion and it will leave some faces stunned, shocked, and surprised. So why the girls are in the washroom talking, another woman overhears their conversation while the three of them are in front of the mirror.

"Excuse me I don't mean to be rude or disrespectful but I couldn't help to overhear y'all conversation and did I hear one of you say that one of the guys at the table was named Dex?"

Alicia looks at Samantha as they both look at the young lady.

"Yea, why and what's it to you." Alicia says.

"Is that short for Dexter?"

"Yes, and what's with all the questions?" Samantha says to the lady as she gets irritated with all the questions she is asking.

"Oh, nothing, enjoy the rest of your night." she grins and walks out the washroom laughing and giggling.

So as soon as the washroom door closes Alicia and Samantha look at each other with this suspicious look on their face, then Samantha storms out of the washroom walking toward the young lady.

"Excuse me, can I talk to you for a minute?" Alicia says as the young lady smiles and laughs as she turns around and starts walking towards Samantha and Alicia.

"I'm sorry, I'm Sam."

"And I'm Alicia, would you like to come join us at our table for some drinks?"

"Sure, let me get my coat and I'll be over there shortly, by the way, I'm Lisa."

"Okay Lisa, we're at the table over by the bar."

"By the shimmery statue right?"

"Yes, the shiny one lol."

"Okay," she laughs.

"Okay see you in a little while," as Samantha walks away smiling and Alicia is grinning ear to ear.

Meanwhile, the fellas go into the washroom, but they are in and out. So, heading to the table Dex sees a familiar face, it is the young lady that Alicia and Samantha were talking to in the washroom, and she is heading to their table.

"Oh, hell no, are you fuckin serious?" Dex says in shock.

But by the time he can react she is already seated.

"Everyone this is Lisa, Lisa this is everyone." Alicia says.

"This is my boo Choice, over there is Adam, Mr. Reynolds to my left and this is Dex." Samantha says as Dex looks like he sees a ghost, Lisa smiles, giggles and laughs and says, "Hello everyone."

"So, Lisa where are you from?" Alicia asks.

"Memphis, but I been living here for a couple of years now."

"What part of Memphis you from?" Samantha asks.

"East Memphis."

"That's what up, well we have some drinks help yourself."

"Okay, but the waiter is bringing my drink over here."

"Okay, well we were playing questions, so feel free to listen then jump in if you want to."

"Oh, okay that sounds fun, and jump in I will."

Mr. Reynolds hasn't stop smiling since Lisa came over and sits down at the table and Dex hasn't stop looking like he is thinking hard plus pissed off.

"Okay, a heads up and for the record, if you all didn't know I use to mess around with Dex a couple of years ago, and I use to work with Mr. Reynolds as well. So, if none of you knew that either."

Sam smiles hard and laughs, then claps with more laughter as Alicia sips her drink and smiles.

"Oh, wow now that should make this interesting." Adam says after looking around.

Alicia starts laughing.

"And the plot thickens." Mr. Reynolds says as he smirks and pours him another glass of Stella then signals the waiter so she can bring another pitcher over.

Now everyone sits there with the shit face, except for Mr. Reynolds, because he knows who she is before she even sat down, and he had an idea what she is about to bring up as well.

Then everyone looks at Sam and Alicia, while Lisa sips her drink and smiles.

"So Dex, would you like to tell everyone our history or would you want me to tell them?"

"Idgaf what you tell them I just want to know why the fuck are you here."

Everyone looks shocks, as Alicia and Samantha give each other a high five.

"Oh, he big mad." Samantha says as Alicia giggles.

"You know what, don't worry about it, I think I should just leave."

"Wait, why you leaving, girl fuck him and sit down." Alicia says.

"Obviously, I'm not wanted here, so why should I be here."

"No stay, fuck Dex he doesn't know nothing here, but that big ass lip, sit down girl." Samantha says.

"Yes, stay I want this back and forth between the two of you all to end today plus this is great entertainment." Mr. Reynolds says as he pulls out his cigar.

"Okay here goes." Lisa says as the waiter brings her a double shot of Remy.

"First, I know all these guys very well." Lisa says as Alicia looks at Adam and puts her hands on her waist, Sam looks at Choice and folds her arms, while Dex looks pissed and Mr. Reynolds grins.

"Is, that so, please continue."

"Yea, Lisa finish." Alicia says as she looks at Adam.

"Okay, so I'm a call girl."

"Oh, hell naw, WTF." Samantha says.

"Are you fucking serious?" Alicia says as the table gets quiet.

"And each one of these guys have paid for my services before, some on more than one occasion."

"You got to be shitting me but keep talking hoe."

Tension at the table is at an all-time high now.

Samantha balls her fist up and starts to crack her knuckles, as Lisa looks at her, laughs, and continues to tell the story.

"Okay, it started with Adam a couple of times, we met at the bar and fucked that same night in his car and after that, we got a room at the motel 6 every week, he told me he wanted to be my king, so I let him, he paid, and we played, a whole lot. Then, he put me onto Dex who I was in a full relationship with because he said he really liked me and didn't want me doing this job, so I stopped to be committed and dedicated to our relationship, but as time went on he was unhappy so after a couple of months we decided to go our separate ways. But I had seen Choice with them a couple of times before, then I saw him at the club one night all by his-self, we talked and had drinks, the next thing I know we was in a room having sex. Now Mr. Reynolds on the other hand he was like a father figure to me because the time I and his son was together, we had several conversations, about a lot of stuff. He also told me Dex wasn't ready for a relationship, but I didn't listen I had to learn the hard way."

"Call girl huh, so they were paying you for sex, must be some good pussy."

"You feel me, either that or it's made of diamonds wait, you said all three of them was paying you?"

"Yes."

Samantha crosses her arms

"Oh okay."

So, as everybody looks around to see Adam and Choice drinking and Dex sucking on that ice full of so much rage he starts biting the ice.

"So y'all sorry ass paying for pussy huh okay, is this true Adam?"

"I am not answering that question because it sounds like it's more questions where that one came from."

"You guys need to be careful of the stuff you are getting into because you fellas have some good women. Adam, Alicia is a great woman; you should have been a better man to her. Dex, you had a good woman in Samantha, but you let her get away with your selfish ways. And Choice you have a good woman so get your shit together."

Then everybody starts shouting, yelling, and screaming, then Lisa gets everyone's attention,

"Hold up, wait a fucking minute, that's not it so y'all need to chill out and let me finish."

"Bitch fuck you! I should whoop your ass, for not telling us this earlier when we were in the washroom when we were talking to your funky ass." Samantha says in rage.

Then Alicia tries to get up and go over to fight Lisa, but she is pushed back by Adam, then she punches his ass in the jaw.

"Sit your dumbass down motherfukker." Alicia says as Adam falls in his seat then sits there while holding his cheek.

Meanwhile Choice tries to get up and leave.

"Where the fuck you going buddy, sit your dumb ass down."

"Girl get the fuck out of here girl, you fucked her husband but you trying to tell me what to do, better get your life together and leave me the fukk alone." He says as he stands up and fixes his clothes then sits down.

"Wait a minute y'all chill, I want to know what else she has to say, finish Lisa."

Lisa looks at Mr. Reynolds as he massages his cigar.

"Don't look over there at Mr. Reynolds he can't help you, talk bitch."

"Spill the beans hoe, before I do you like I just did Adam."

"For the record, I used protection with everyone, but I and Dex stop using it after 3 months into the relationship. But I noticed that none of them even seemed to know the difference from the sex. And since no one knew the difference, so I left it alone. And my other confession is that I paid a lot of money, for my booty, my titties, and my penis tuck before I transitioned."

Dex throws up in his mouth, Choice throws his glass at her, and Adam tries to grab her by the neck, but Mr. Reynolds grabs him. Alicia and Samantha look at each other and starts crying laughing.

Mr. Reynolds laughs and pours him another glass of beer.

"Hell naw, lol y'all need to do a pussy check before y'all decide to cheat fellas."

"With y'all dumb gay asses lmao." Alicia says as she pours her a glass of the champagne.

"That's what the fuck they get, fukking dummies." Samantha says while laughing as sh sips her drink.

So, Lisa gets up leaves out and leaves $50 tip on the table, walks out while Mr. Reynolds still laughing.

"And for the record just because it looks good, doesn't mean it is." Mr. Reynolds says as he watches everyone get up and leave out, then he sits back and flames up his cigar, and laughs before Lisa comes walking pass from coming from the washroom.

"The liquor ran through you huh, lol."

"Oh, Mr. Reynolds I thought you left with everyone else."

"Naw I wanted to finish my cigar before I left."

"By the way I wanted to talk to you about something."

"Have a seat, waiter can we get another bottle of that chardonnay please."

"Coming right up Mr. Reynolds."

"You must be a regular in here if they know you by your name." Lisa says as she sits down.

"A little more than a regular, I actually own the place." He says as Lisa looks shocked as the waiter brings the wine and she sits down.

"So what did you want to talk to me about?"

....to be continued

Coming soon 2021

Sudoku volume 2

Crossword volume 2

You are single until you're married 2: Love is pain

Sex assassin 2: Pleasured punishment

Romantic war 2: Love and war

Bullets talk

Tears of sin

Kool-aid corner (childrens book)

Malfunction

Poetic Journey

Recycled pain

Love coward

Four wheels(childrens book)

Town of lies

Wild thoughts

Sheet puller

Broke state of mind

www.ingramcontent.com/pod-product-compliance
Lightning Source LLC
Chambersburg PA
CBHW071159130626
46555CB00004B/1514